LI🦁N Lion

Miriam Busch

Illustrated by

Larry Day

SCHOLASTIC INC.

New York Toronto London Auckland Sydney New Delhi Hong Kong

To Larry,
who leaps into
the lion's jaws
with me.
And to Anne,
Laura, and
Christine, who
shine rescue
torches.
—M.B.

To Miriam,
who fills my life
with color
—L.D.

Lion!

The artist used watercolor, gouache, Wolff pencil, and pencil on Twinrocker handmade watercolor paper to create the illustrations for this book.
Typography and cover design by Martha Rago.

Text copyright © 2014 by Miriam Busch.
Illustrations copyright © 2014 by Larry Day.
All rights reserved. Published by Scholastic Inc., 557 Broadway, New York, NY 10012, by arrangement with HarperCollins Children's Books, a division of HarperCollins Publishers.
Printed in the U.S.A.

ISBN-13: 978-0-545-86308-7 ISBN-10: 0-545-86308-2

SCHOLASTIC and associated logos are trademarks and/or registered trademarks of Scholastic Inc.

9 10   40   24 23 22 21 20

Lion!

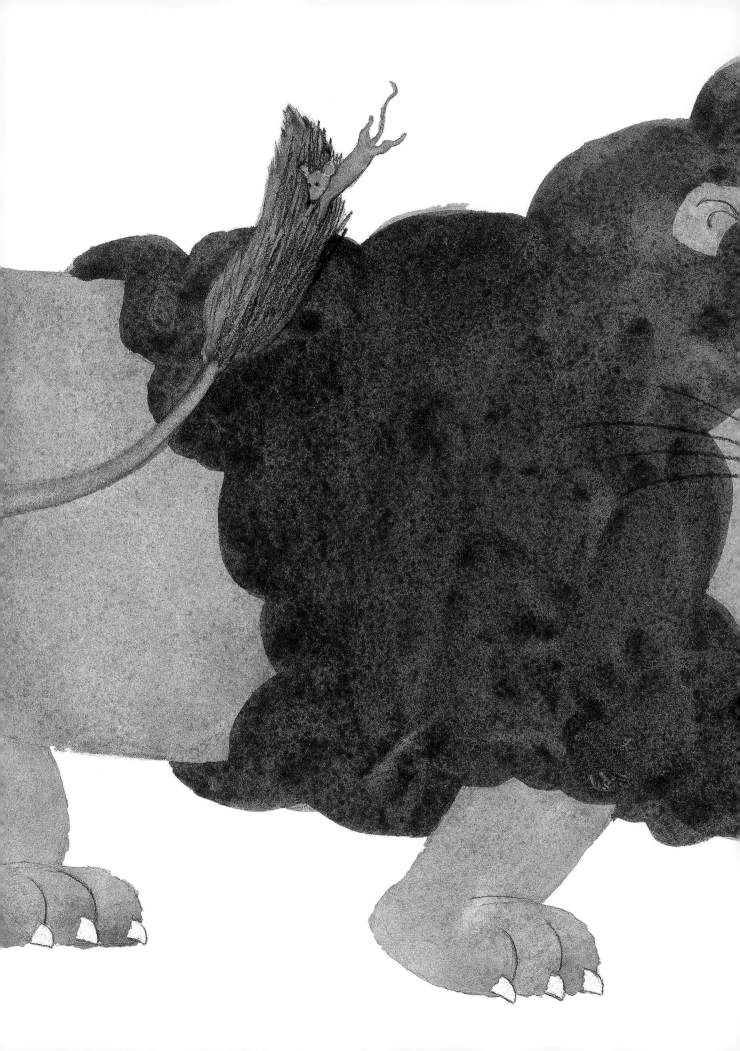

What are you doing?

Trying to find Lion.
What about you?

I'm looking for lunch.

Lunch?
Care for some grass?

**No.
Too snappy.**

Snappy?

Ah, I see.
Maybe a mushroom?

**No.
Too prickly!**

Do you
like berries?
Ripe and
delicious.

**No.
Too stinky.**

Hmm. Snappy, prickly, stinky, you say?

How about seeds?

NO.

Well, then.
Flowers?

No!

NO!

No!

Feathers make me sneeze.

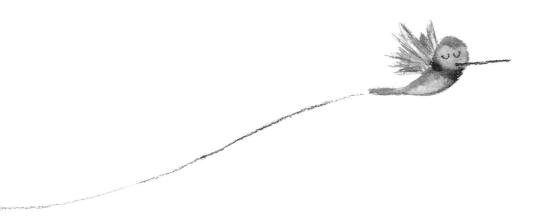

Sneeze? You don't say.

Lion must be very hungry now.
Let's bring him home.

Don't worry, Lion!

Mew!

There you are, Lion!

Ah...

ahh...

ahhh...

Lion!

Mew!